BISCOTTI AND BETRAYAL

A BELLE HARBOR COZY MYSTERY (BOOK 10)

SUE HOLLOWELL

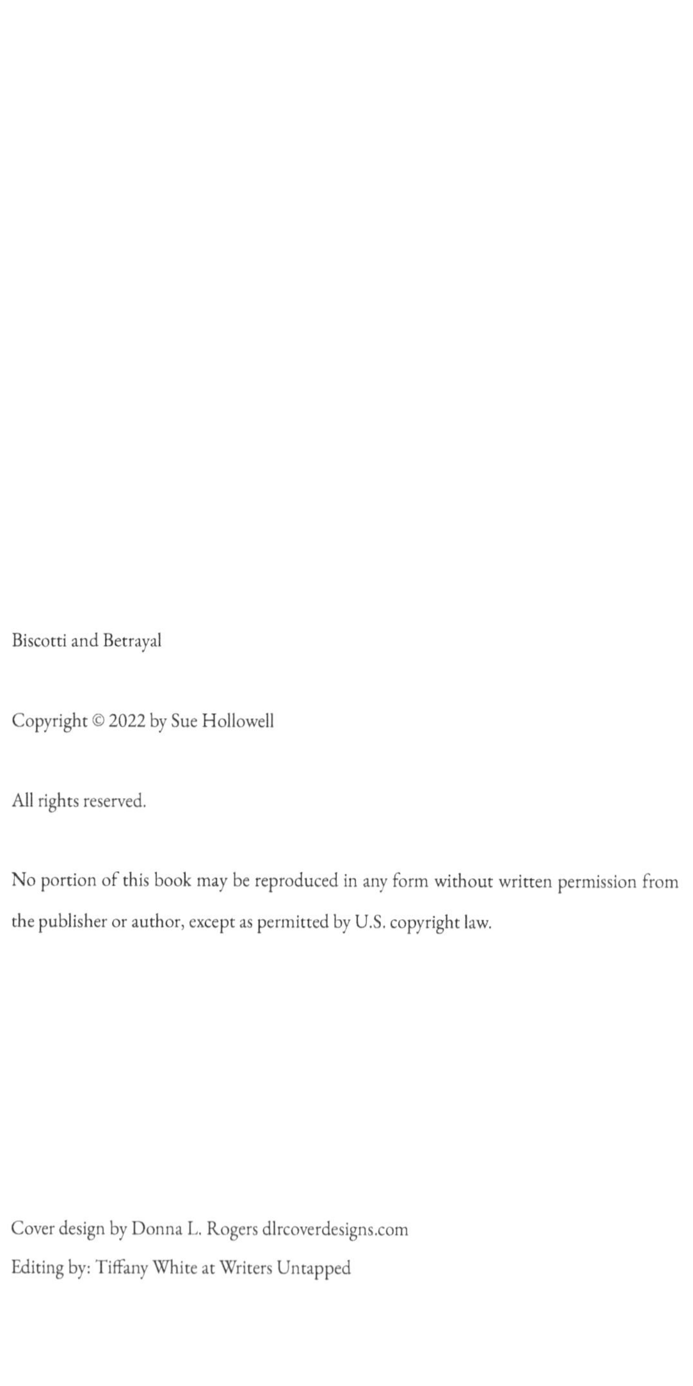

Biscotti and Betrayal

Copyright © 2022 by Sue Hollowell

All rights reserved.

No portion of this book may be reproduced in any form without written permission from the publisher or author, except as permitted by U.S. copyright law.

Cover design by Donna L. Rogers dlrcoverdesigns.com

Editing by: Tiffany White at Writers Untapped

CONTENTS

CHAPTER ONE

The Evergreen trees towered over both sides of us, providing little light on our path. Thankfully, Justin had convinced me to acquire a pair of hiking shoes to support my feet as we traversed the tree-root and rocky-lined dirt path. The day would no doubt develop into a classic weather beauty for Belle Harbor, but for now the coolness meant small bugs were out in force. Long sleeves would keep me from getting eaten up by the critters, but I was already getting pretty warm.

Justin led the way along the McLane Creek Nature Trail as I quietly trailed behind. The brochure promised at the turn of this four-mile hike that we would be at a lookout to oversee the cliffs hundreds of feet above the ocean. At the moment, it felt as if we would never emerge from the forest.

Turning and holding out his hand, Justin asked, "Do you need to take a break for a bit?" He gestured toward a bench along the path. The hike until now had been relatively easy, and since I had taken up running, my endurance had significantly improved.

"Nah, I'm good. You?" I smiled. Justin could probably sprint the entire length of the trail and still have wind left over. He kept himself in shape with a lot of water activities, namely surfing. He vowed one day he would get me on a board. I wasn't so sure. Actually, I was very sure that wouldn't happen, but that didn't keep him from trying to convince me. We had done stand-up paddle boarding on a recent trip. Kneeling in a still body of water was still a challenge for me. I didn't see how I could stand up when waves were carrying me forward.

We continued our silent trek. The fresh air cleared my head from recent events so I could concentrate on planning Uncle Jack and Linda's wedding. Everything about it needed to be perfect for those two. There was no more deserving couple than Unkie and Linda for a magical experience of sending them off in wedded bliss, and I would do whatever I could to make that happen. The songbirds in the thick of the woods serenaded us on our travels, the therapy of nature again providing just what I needed. Uncle Jack had insisted that I go with Justin on this hike, even volunteering to get up before dawn to assist Linda in our daily baking. He might regret that later when he was ready for bed by three p.m. Though giving him an opportunity to spend more time with Linda was not a chore for him. Those two were so in love, even baking before the sun came up was a romantic event for them.

By my calculations, we should be nearing the summit of our hike and the rewarding view for our effort. Stopping in front of me, Justin turned, pulling the trail map from his pocket.

"What's wrong?" I asked, joining him, looking at the map.

He pointed toward the left, an overgrown trail with vines, leaves, and twigs covering it like a blanket. "I think that's the turn we're supposed to take, but it's not cleared out." He bowed his head over the map, pivoted, and held it out in front of him like a divining rod he hoped to guide our way.

Turning to the path on the right, I said, "Seems like they made a mistake." The trail in front of me was clear of debris, like our route so far had been.

"Maybe we should take a break and regroup," Justin said, plopping onto the bench set apart from the trail.

Was he just being considerate to make sure I didn't poop out? We weren't even at the halfway point, but I felt great. And the incline was very slight, raising my confidence I could easily make the entire trail without stopping. Humoring him, I said, "OK," sitting beside him, opening my water bottle to take a swig.

"Have you been on this trail before?" I asked, tucking my water bottle into the outside pocket of my backpack.

"Not this one specifically. But others in this system. And the maps are always accurate," he said, folding the paper and sticking it into his pocket. "I think we should follow the clear path."

I shrugged. "OK." Why was this bothering him so much? "Do you want to tag along to visit the wedding venue?" Maybe changing the subject would loosen up this normally very relaxed guy.

"Maybe," he replied, slowly turning to grin at me.

My face warmed up, suspecting the intent behind his tone. We had been going out officially only a few months, even though we had been friends for longer. It was so easy to be with Justin, and he regularly coaxed me out of my shell. He supported me in my crazy endeavors and allowed me to be myself, not trying to mold me into any vision he might have for his girlfriend. I could truly see myself with Justin for the rest of my life, but I couldn't let my emotions get too far ahead of my rational brain.

Vaulting from the bench, I headed down the clear path, trying to shake off the anxiety like a smashed avocado stuck to my hand.

"Tilly," Justin hollered.

Slowing my pace, I turned to see him jog up to me.

He grabbed my hand, saying, "We'll take things at the speed comfortable for you." Knowing he didn't mean our hike, I pondered how in the world he was so perceptive to my thoughts and behavior. Was I that outward in expressing myself? Another beautiful example of how he supported me. Ahh, Justin.

Silently, we strode side by side, making our way toward the clearing ahead of us and the prize for our work. The brochure depicted a bench at the lookout, overseeing cliffs that led down to the ocean and a view similar to that of the winery we had visited on the Coast Excursion train, making you feel like you were on top of the world.

Emerging into the opening felt like finally taking a deep breath after holding it for several minutes. The scenery was as advertised, but I looked around for the promised seating. We had planned to rest and eat our lunch before winding our way back down to the trailhead.

"Where's the bench?" I asked, wandering around the clearing, as if expecting to find it hidden under shrubbery.

Justin pulled the paper out again and studied it, shaking his head. "I'm going to have to talk to the county parks department. What they've got in here"—he tapped the pamphlet—"isn't even close." He stepped to the edge of the clearing and held his arms out to the side. "But it's still stunning."

The birds continued to sing sweet little songs as I joined Justin to gaze at the sweeping Vista. "We can just use our jackets to sit on while we eat," I suggested.

I turned to scout out a spot and halted at the obnoxious sound of screeching tires below us on the coast highway. I returned to the edge and Justin pointed to a dark SUV speeding around the sharp curve, just as it bumped the smaller red car in front of it. My hand flew to my mouth, eyes wide as I felt like I was watching an action movie in slow motion.

"That car is driving recklessly. I think it deliberately hit that other one," he said. As if right on cue, the SUV surged and rammed the smaller car, driving it right off the cliff toward the ocean.

I grabbed Justin's arm. "We have to go see if they're OK."

"Tilly," Justin said. I knew that tone. How could anybody survive that fall? Until I found out for sure, I had to preserve hope.

CHAPTER TWO

Turning and racing down the path we had just come from, Justin led the way at a fast jog. He stopped, shaking his head, his brows furrowed. "It's going to take forever going the way we did on the route up here." He pointed to his left into a thick underbrush. The tree canopy darkened in the direction he showed. "I have to go. Can you see if you can get a signal to call Barney?"

No doubt the police chief needed to investigate, but first we had to see if we had a rescue or a recovery situation on our hands. "Justin, are you sure?"

"The shortest direction between two points…" he started, heading into the shrubbery, picking his way through the vines and bushes. The complicated terrain slowed his pace, but maybe overall it would be a faster route. I hoped his bearings would lead us close to where the car had plunged toward the ocean.

"I'm coming with you," I said, venturing into the forest, the sticker bushes scraping my legs. Stomping after Justin, I lifted my legs high to avoid tripping. His pace quickened, which lengthened the distance between us. Focusing on the forest floor, I attempted to step where there was little underbrush. Why would someone so recklessly navigate those sharp curves, especially near the cliff and with another car right by them? Were they drunk? Did they know the person and were possibly chasing them? Looking ahead, I saw that Justin continued to lengthen his lead. The sun was absent from our sight, preventing us from using it as a guide toward our destination. The only sign we were going in the right direction was the slope of the hill. As long as we were descending, I hoped that was a good sign.

Justin stopped and hollered, "Are you OK?"

I turned and looked behind me. The trail we left was nowhere in view. There was no turning back now. "Yeah," I replied, looking down, my legs now striped light pink. At least I wasn't bleeding yet.

Cupping the sides of his mouth, he yelled, "We're getting to a pretty steep drop off." He pointed the opposite direction.

What did that mean? Were we going to turn around? He waited for me to join him as I peered over the edge. "What do you think?"

"Really, we're probably better off sliding down on our butts, or we risk a pretty nasty fall," he suggested, neither of those two options sounding preferable. "I can see it clears up about halfway down, and we should probably be able to pick up some speed."

Catching my breath, I said, "Let's go for it," and stepped around Justin to continue our travels.

"Tilly, go as slow as you need to," he said, gesturing toward my legs. "You're all scraped up. I am so sorry I got us into this."

"It was my decision. And we need to keep our heads focused on that driver over the cliff. A few scratches on my legs are nothing," I said.

Weaving past me, Justin said, "Let me go first to be the guinea pig." He quietly picked his way through the shrubs for about ten yards and stopped. "The point of no return." The trees overhead were letting in a little more light, confirming we were going the right direction. Gazing down the slope, he said, "If I crouch and lean back a bit, I think I'll make it almost to the bottom. Then I can walk the rest of the way down the hill."

That was as good of a plan as any, and we had little choice. The sound of the cars passing on the road below was getting louder. Did anyone else witness what we had seen? Would there be others helping to rescue the person over the cliff? How would they get there and what would they do when they arrived? I had to call Barney as soon as possible to summon help.

Stepping forward, Justin squatted and sat on the ground, giving himself a shove off toward the bottom, gaining speed and bumping along the way. He quickly leapt to his feet like you would at the bottom of a slide at a park. He turned and yelled up at me, "Your turn. Hug your knees a bit. That helps keep you from tumbling."

Life with Justin was always an adventure, even when one wasn't planned. Following his instructions, I sat, wrapped my arms around my knees, and scooted to the edge for my ride down the hill. As I approached Justin, he held out his hands to halt me from careening further out of control.

"Great job," he said. "I don't think we're too far from the road now."

The underbrush was just as thick as it was at the top of the hill. We high-stepped our way along the last stretch to get to the road. Justin emerged onto the gravel, looking both ways. Cars whizzed by as if they were on a racetrack. The more dangerous part of our journey was ahead as we tried to dodge vehicles to cross the road. Looking both ways, Justin grabbed my hand, and we sprinted to the other side, near a small rock wall that separated us from the steep cliff below. A large portion of the boulders smashed open where the car had veered off the road to the ground below. Now what?

We gazed down the hill toward the small red vehicle for any signs of life. The left rear bumper of the car was smashed, but otherwise the scene looked like a crane had picked it up and set it down at the bottom. No movement. From what I could tell, there was only one person in the car. Pulling out my phone, I called Barney as Justin began navigating down to check out the victim. I closed my eyes as I waited for Barney to answer, hoping that when I opened them, I could report that we had an accident victim that was alive.

Cars continued whizzing behind me as I stepped as close to the edge as possible without skidding down to join Justin.

Shading his eyes, Justin bent to look inside the driver's side window. *Please, please, please.* He yanked the door open and reached a hand inside.

I explained to Barney where we were, and he sent the emergency responders on their way.

Straightening up, Justin looked my direction and shook his head. Oh, that poor person. Who were they and why would that other car run them off the road? I hoped it wouldn't be too difficult to find them once we gave Barney a description. Large, darker SUV. Right front had to have fender damage and maybe even red paint from the car they hit. Was this a case of road rage taken too far?

Justin climbed up the wall of rocks and shrubs to join me in waiting for help to arrive. He wrapped me in a hug. "I'm sorry, Tilly. He's dead."

My muscles relaxed into his embrace. "Why would someone do that?" I mumbled into his shoulder.

Releasing me, Justin grabbed my hand and led us to a place along the road where the rock wall was still intact. We sat in silence, waiting for Barney and the recovery team to arrive. Cars sped by as I was on high alert, hoping with all my might that by chance the killer would drive by.

CHAPTER THREE

T he overhead lights in the bakery kitchen shone brightly as I waited for Dexter to arrive. Several cream-filled cupcakes on a nearby plate quickly disappeared as I gobbled them up, my mind distracted from the events of yesterday. I couldn't get the vision of the car over the cliff and the killer on the loose out of my mind. Would they strike again? What had caused them to target another driver and run them off the road? I scarfed down another cupcake, a sugar high imminent.

My baking partner and Uncle Jack's fiancé quietly performed her kitchen chores, cleaning, packing up muffins and cupcakes for delivery, leaving me to comfort my thoughts with sweets. I shoved the plate away, my teeth about to pop out of my mouth if I ate any more. Trying to channel my energy more productively, I stood and headed to our recipe box. I had offered Dexter the opportunity to learn the baking side of the business. He eagerly agreed and would arrive any minute. Even though he was only hired part-time for deliveries, our resident teenager yearned for more responsibility. With the right attitude, I believed people could do almost anything they put their mind to. And I primed Dexter for the next step.

I retrieved the simplest recipe I could find, and one that, if it wasn't perfect, would still turn out well. Morning muffins. These goodies were one of the best sellers we provided to Mocha Joe's Coffee Shop and were a great complement to his signature coffee drinks. No matter that when I first made them, considering that they had bran in them, Unkie had bristled at what he called *poop producers*. Coupled with the fact there were vegetables in the mix, carrots, I'm surprised he tried them at all. It was only because the flavor disguised the healthy parts.

"Hey boss," Dexter said, loping over to my side with his lanky frame. "Ready for my training."

Placing my hand on my heart, I breathed in to slow my breath from Dexter's startling entry. That kid was always upbeat and full of energy, ready to try anything. "OK," I said, peering over his shoulder at Linda snickering behind a towel held in front of her face. Dexter had only been hired a short time ago, but we couldn't imagine this business without him.

"You seem kinda jumpy," he said.

Fiddling with the recipe card, running my hand along the smooth lamination, I said, "Yeah, something horrible happened yesterday, and I can't get it out of my head."

"Oh no, boss. I'm sorry." His bushy brows furrowed with concern. Looking back at Linda, he said, "Anything I can do to help?"

"No, I think our baking therapy will be sufficient," I replied, handing him the card. "How about you take the lead and I guide you through the steps?" I suggested.

Standing tall, he bent his arm and poised his hand, saluting me. "I'm ready to learn," he said.

If I could clone that kid... "Step one, preparation. If you properly set yourself up in the beginning, you'll have a much easier time later." I pulled a stool next to the kitchen counter workspace and plopped down. "This is kind of fun. Sitting here, barking out orders."

Linda and Dexter chuckled.

"Gather your ingredients and place them in the sequence you'll need them," I said.

Linda interjected, "I'll peel the carrots for you." I loved my little team. The chemistry of our crew provided such a joyous workplace. My reluctance to mess with something that was working well made it hard to search for new employees.

Retrieving measuring cups and spoons and laying them out in order according to the recipe, Dexter asked, "So what happened yesterday?" He headed to the dry goods storage to get out the flour, sugar, soda, bran, and flax seeds.

Maybe talking through it would help break a block in my brain. My thoughts fixated on the sight of the car over the cliff. "Justin and I were on a hike when we heard this horrific sound of tires squealing and a crash." I shuddered, reliving the chaos and confusion.

"Oh no," Dexter said, squeezing the flour bag so hard it emitted an immense cloud of dust that covered his shirt.

Handing him an apron to prevent further damage to his attire, I said, "We saw a car deliberately run someone off the road."

Pausing, I wrung my hands.

"Are they OK?" he asked. A logical question, and one I didn't want to face.

I closed my eyes and shook my head. "No. Sadly."

"I'm sorry, Tilly," he said, turning to focus on measuring out the ingredients. Maybe talking to him, especially with something so emotional, was a bad idea on his first baking excursion. I really wanted this to go well for him.

I retrieved the wet ingredients for him and placed the eggs and applesauce nearby as Linda completed grating the carrots.

"The weird thing, Dexter, is that the SUV intentionally crashed into the smaller car. Like they planned to run them off the road," I said. "Justin climbed down the embankment to check on the person, but they didn't make it."

Loading the wet ingredients into the mixer, Dexter turned it on low to blend. "Was it someone you knew?"

"No," I said. "It was a small red car with a guy in it. The other one was a large, darker SUV."

Dexter spun toward me, his eyes wide. "Did it have a sticker on it that said *Hang 10*?"

Wracking my brain for the details, I said, "I don't think so. Why?"

Dexter stood still. "My friend Colin has a car that sounds like that," he said.

I moved over to the mixer and turned it off, our baking tutorial coming to a halt. "Dexter, call him to make sure he's OK. I'm pretty sure it didn't have that sticker." But I couldn't be certain. My attention had been on the driver, not the car.

Dexter moved aside and pulled out his phone. He paused before he started typing out a message. It may not have been Dexter's friend, but it was *someone's* friend and family member in that crash. Seeing the despair on that young man's face angered me. Why would someone take such senseless action to ram a car over a cliff?

Holding his phone down at his side, he waited for a response as he paced through the kitchen. "I can't remember the last time I heard from Colin," he said, running his hand through his thick curly hair, causing it to stand on end.

"Don't let your mind go there," I encouraged. "Take one step at a time."

"I texted Colin's sister Kayla," he mumbled, looking down at his phone as if willing it to respond.

Linda stepped in to finish preparing the batch of muffins. There would be plenty of time in the future for training.

"Dexter, why don't we assemble some boxes while you wait for a reply?" I said, trying to distract him with mundane tasks.

"Huh?" he said, gazing at his phone. "Oh, yeah, OK."

I pulled down a stack of twenty boxes from the shelf and handed half of them to Dexter. I began folding, trying to get him to follow my lead.

He stood frozen, nothing deterring his focus from his phone until he got an answer.

I continued folding as his buzzing phone echoed.

"I'm afraid to look," he said, handing the phone to me.

I was afraid to look, too, but there wasn't anything I wouldn't do for this kid. Linda stepped forward as I turned the phone to see the response. Releasing my breath, I said, "It wasn't Colin. Kayla heard about the crash, but it wasn't him," I said.

Dexter wrapped me up in a bear hug and twirled me around. "Tilly, so sorry," he said, wiping his brow. "I'm just so relieved, I got carried away."

"It's OK, Dexter. I'm glad your friend is OK." The sad truth was that somebody's friend wasn't OK, and I needed to find answers.

CHAPTER FOUR

The wind blew my hair from my face as Fiona drove along the scenic coast highway. She insisted I get away for a change of scenery before I stress ate the entire bakery. We were headed to Diamond Hills to check out a spa she had been wanting to visit. Thankfully, my friend wouldn't take no for an answer. Just hearing her description of all the amenities made me relax. A day of pampering would be heavenly. And it usually took someone else to force me to spend time on myself. Definitely an area of improvement for me.

I held my arm out the window, air surfing, daydreaming about spa treatments, facials, manicures, and massages. The more I thought about it, the more committed I got to making it happen.

"Thank you for dragging me out," I said, chuckling. "Somehow you always know what I need and at just the right time."

"You got it, my friend," Fiona replied. "But I think it's going to take more than a drive to dislodge that worry from your face."

Shaking my head, I said, "I just can't get the sound of tires screeching out of my head."

"Isn't it just up around the corner that it happened?" Fiona gestured toward the front of the car.

"Yeah, about half a mile," I replied. She was right. Until I had answers, my mind wouldn't let go of the horror of the scene, and the senseless move of the SUV driver to shove the other car off the road. Forcefully causing my brain to change subjects, I said, "I just love this car." Fiona's little VW bug was cute and a fun vehicle. Her wheel covers were in the shape of daisies, and her antenna was a daisy stem with a flower at the top.

"Why don't you get one? We could be twinsies!" she said, tapping the steering wheel in laughter.

"I'm pretty sure you're serious, but I don't really need it," I replied as she slowed near the crash site. My head swiveled to the left side of the road, where Justin and I had slid down the hill, then to the right, where the broken rock wall showed where the car had gone over. I turned further to the right in my seat as we passed by to see it from another angle.

"Need isn't the point, Tilly," Fiona said. "You're making good money at the bakery, and you never do anything to enjoy the results of your hard work."

"I agreed to go to the spa," I said, grinning.

"OK, baby steps," she said. "You left Boston to live your life on your terms. Don't miss the opportunity."

I needed Fiona to push me. Changing my mindset was a work in progress. Since arriving in Belle Harbor I had accomplished a ton of what I wanted to do, namely opening Luna's Bakery and Cafe in honor of my grandmother. But I couldn't stop there. She was right. What was life, if not an adventure? And I could hear Unkie's voice in my head, too, echoing Fiona's advice. It might not be a car yet, but I vowed to stretch from my comfort zone more often.

Fiona glanced in her rear-view mirror as the rumble of a large engine got closer. Glancing down at the speedometer, she said, "What's this guy's problem? I'm not going to speed any more through these winding curves."

A horn blared behind us as the SUV roared to our left side and dove in front of the bug, speeding away. Taking her foot off the gas, Fiona swore. "Can you believe that jerk?"

Pointing after the vehicle as it disappeared around corners, I said, "I think that was him! He was going so fast, I can't be sure, but I think his right front bumper was dented with some red paint on it from the car he hit." My heart raced at the thought that we could have been his next victims.

Fiona tightly gripped the steering wheel and sped up. "Let's see if we can follow him," she suggested.

And then what? If he was angry enough to use his vehicle as a weapon, what would we encounter if we met him in person?

Rounding the next corner, we spotted him up ahead on the tail of the car in front of him, laying on the horn. I closed my eyes, hoping he also passed them by without an incident. Oncoming traffic prevented him from going around the car as he continued pounding the horn. Speed limit signs instructed us to slow down as we neared the small town of Merbeach Landing. Instead of going around the car on the highway, the SUV took a hard right toward town. This couldn't be good. At this time of day, a lot of tourists would be out walking around, enjoying the shops, and I knew from Belle Harbor they didn't always pay much attention to the cars as they were crossing the road. This guy could do a lot of damage in a small amount of time.

Fiona turned on her blinker and followed him down the road into town. He zigzagged past the slower-moving vehicles, gaining distance from us.

"Fiona, should we call the cops or something?" I asked, feeling completely helpless to save unsuspecting pedestrians from this road menace.

She sat forward in her seat, intently focused as she looked left and right down side streets to spot the vehicle. "Where could he have gone?" She pulled into the beach park parking lot at the end of the road and turned the car facing away from the ocean. Pounding the steering wheel, she said, "It's only a matter of time before he does more damage. Did you get a good look?"

"I didn't get the license plate, but I think I got the description." I pulled my backpack from the back seat and retrieved my ever-present notebook and pen. SUV, charcoal, or dark gray. Four doors with a roof rack on top. Right front damage. Other than the last part, that account sounded like pretty much every other SUV on the road and not much more information than I got from the first time I saw him. Maybe if we drove that stretch of highway enough, we could get another look, but at what cost?

"Maybe we should call it a day," Fiona suggested.

"Agreed. Although if there were ever a time we needed a spa day, it would be right now," I said, chuckling, trying to release some tension.

Fiona turned and pointed at me. "I'm taking that as a commitment. When we get back home, the first thing we're doing is checking our calendars and booking an appointment for the works."

That sounded heavenly, and I needed no more convincing.

Shifting the car into gear, Fiona slowly exited the parking lot, reversing our route from town out to the highway. How in the world would I ever get enough detail on this guy to catch him? Or at least provide the information to Barney. If he got wind of Fiona and me giving chase, he would have our hides.

CHAPTER FIVE

"Tilly, I wish you would have at least brought a light jacket," Uncle Jack said from the front passenger seat of Linda's car. We were on our way to meet with the event coordinator at the mountain lodge where Linda wanted to have their wedding ceremony. The scenery was eerily similar to that on the hike Justin and I recently did, reminding me of unanswered questions. Large evergreen trees that must have been hundreds of years old towered on both sides of the road. The winding road would take us about an hour out of town to a fairly high elevation that was almost guaranteed to have the snow Linda desired on the day of the wedding.

"Yeah, I figured we'd be inside most of the time. Plus, I have little cold weather gear," I said. I left behind as much of my former life as possible in Boston. And that included all the extra layers needed for several months of the year. The temperature in Belle Harbor was so consistent that I could wear the same outfit 365 days a year.

Turning in his seat, Unkie said, "I can pretty much guess where your mind is at." There was no doubt. Previously, I had made progress in gathering clues with my system of diagramming out the victim, motives, and relationships the victim had with prospective suspects. But this murder appeared to be so random I couldn't figure out which direction to go. Maybe if I just started my drawing, it would trigger a new thought. Worth a try. Pulling out my notebook, I flipped to a fresh page and wrote *Allen* in the middle circle. I had learned the name from one of the first responders at the scene while Justin and I waited for the recovery process. Justin humored me and we stayed until I could find out everything possible before we headed home the day of our fateful hike.

I drew several lines out from Allen's name with empty circles. On one line I wrote road rage as a motive and SUV in the circle. "Do either of you know anything about Allen?" I asked Unkie and Linda.

Looking at Linda, then back at me, Uncle Jack said, "I know he worked as a mechanic at that place on Bellmont."

Writing mechanic, I noted next to it that maybe the person had received faulty work on their vehicle or poor customer service. Maintaining a car wasn't cheap and they may have been overcharged.

Linda slowed as we approached a long driveway leading to the massive lodge at the top of the hill. On my right was an open field leading to mountainous, jagged peaks. No snow in sight, yet. On my left was a lake surrounded by benches, tables, and several small row boats. I could already feel my blood pressure dropping from the peaceful scenery. Making a mental note, and hearing Fiona's advice in my head to do more things for myself, I added this to my list of adventures for Justin and me.

Driving through the circular driveway to a gravel lot, Linda parked, and we piled out of the car. The fresh air overwhelmed me as I stood and stretched my cramped muscles, vowing to be present for this experience.

"Linda, this is beautiful. I can't imagine a more enchanting place for a wedding," I said.

Joining us from the expansive wrap-around deck, a man greeted, "Hello. I'm Jimmy."

Linda beamed, and I was certain whatever she decided today would be exactly what Uncle Jack would do.

We introduced ourselves, and Jimmy turned, leading us back toward the lodge.

Sweeping his arm around, he said, "I thought we could tour the outside first, then head in to talk more details and catering."

I pulled out my phone to capture some photos to share with Justin. The more I saw of the place, the more convinced I was we had to book a weekend getaway. Around the corner to our right, the deck next to the lodge opened up to include several gas fireplaces and tables, a gorgeous setting where guests could mingle, eat, and stay warm at the same time. My hand flew to my mouth as I stopped in my tracks. Pointing to a few cars in another lot, I asked Jimmy, "Who owns that red car?" Realizing how abrupt my question was, I continued, "I'm sorry. There was a crash yesterday with a very similar car." My stomach churned as it nagged me for some food. The left rear of the small car was damaged identically as Allen's.

Looking at Uncle Jack and Linda as if to get answers to my odd behavior, Jimmy replied, "That belongs to our chef, Monica." Continuing our way to the deck and up the stairs, he continued, "A car ran her off the road several months ago. Never figured out who did it. Why?"

Not wanting to usurp the entire purpose of our visit, I said, "I saw a similar car in a wreck yesterday. Must have been someone different."

Relieving me of any further explanation, Jimmy continued his orientation. "We will have this outdoor seating set up with the fireplaces going. Frankly, it's a more popular spot even when it's cold and snowing than the massive stone fireplace we have inside." Opening the door, we followed him inside. He wasn't kidding. The fireplace to our left from floor to ceiling must have been thirty feet tall.

Linda grabbed Unkie's hand and pulled him close. "Oh, Jack," was all she said, giggling.

Grinning from ear to ear, Jimmy continued, "That's usually the reaction we get." Moving to the hearth with his back to the fireplace, he said, "Most couples have the ceremony here. We move the furniture out so that we've got guest seating. We're pretty flexible."

Looping her arm through Unkie's, Linda continued, "It will be a small ceremony. Do you have an outdoor space that would be possible for the ceremony?"

Jimmy wove his way around the room to the wall of windows overlooking the mountains. "On this side of the lodge we have a wider deck that would work well for that."

"Can you promise my lady some snow to top it off?" Uncle Jack asked, chuckling.

"We haven't disappointed yet," Jimmy said.

"Oh, Jack. It's perfect," Linda said, moving closer to the windows.

"We've got our buffet sampler ready when you are," Jimmy said, heading toward the dining tables. A petite woman with a short black bob entered from a swinging door, carrying a platter of biscotti. "Everyone, this is Monica, our acclaimed chef." Jimmy introduced us all as we sat to sample the feast before us. "One of her specialties is the many flavors of biscotti. We actually sell them worldwide."

Monica distributed small plates to each of us as she described each course. I couldn't wait for this wedding. Forcing my brain to focus on the food, I tried to interject periodic comments. But really this was Linda and Uncle Jack's show. What was it about Monica and her car that fit the scenario exactly as the events from yesterday? Could it be a total coincidence that the same type of car had identical damage? It was highly inappropriate to quiz Monica about it right now. How could I arrange to meet up with her again to quiz her and hopefully reveal more pieces to this bizarre puzzle?

CHAPTER SIX

The evening sun shone over the water, at least an hour before it would sink into the horizon. I laced up my running shoes as I sat on a bench along the boardwalk, bracing myself for some stiff muscles tomorrow. My routine of jogging frequently was interrupted by life events. A convenient excuse, but I needed to remember that I always felt better after my runs.

Standing and stretching my legs, I prepared to head toward the lighthouse at the north end of the beach. I had committed to a shorter run to ease me back into the practice. My plan was to run the board-walk on the way down, then move to the hard sand on the way back to give me more of a challenge. Hugging the right side of the path, I slowly began my jog.

I smiled to myself as my heart grew two sizes, thinking of the joy on Linda's and Unkie's faces yesterday at the wedding venue. The setting was the perfect backdrop for romance and starting their life together beautifully. The coordinator had thought of almost everything so that all we had to do was show up. Along with the food menu, they decorated with an assortment of flowers and, to top it off, strung soft white lights around the room. I got goosebumps just thinking about the day. I only hoped I wouldn't be a blubbering pile of goo by the end of the ceremony.

My plodding steps had taken me about halfway to the turnaround. The back of my thighs made themselves known with a little soreness. Perhaps a warm Epsom salt bath tonight to convince my legs that I didn't intend to torture them.

Nearing the end of the path, I glanced at Fiona's bar to my right, the last business in our little string of shops bordering the beach. Per normal, it was hopping with music pouring out of the open door and a line snaked around the corner. I needed some time with my bestie to help me sort through the clues or, more appropriately, the lack of clues. The act Justin and I witnessed was deliberate. But the why nagged at my brain.

Weaving through the few people in front of me, I made the turn and moved to the sand, my legs feeling heavier. I considered slowing to a walk but toughed it out. As long as the sensation was only discomfort and not pain, I would continue to push myself.

Was it just a wild coincidence that the car at the lodge was almost identical to the one we saw pushed off the cliff? Possibly, but I couldn't let it slide until I knew for sure.

Trudging along the sand, I told myself I was almost done with my run, hoping my thoughts would convince my legs to be kind. That this was the best for my entire body, mind, and soul. I spotted the bench ahead where I had started my jaunt, vowing to make it that far, then rest before heading home.

Would the scenery in Belle Harbor ever get old? The consistency of the temperature, the predictability of the tide, and the beauty were still relatively new to me. I vowed never to take it for granted.

Stopping at the bench, I stretched my arms high and to my sides, bending to flex all muscles. Kindly, at least at the moment, they were cooperating with me. Walking the rest of the way home would provide me a nice cool down.

My life in Belle Harbor couldn't have been more perfect. I was getting better at choosing happiness for myself and the result was wondrous. Prioritizing my needs resulted in being a happier, more content human being, which meant I could be a better person for those in my life. It had taken me some time to reconcile in my head that I didn't need to sacrifice everything for others in order to keep the peace. There was still a hesitation when deciding for myself felt extravagant. And I didn't always get it right, but I was committed to exercising that preference muscle more often to get used to it.

The bakery lights were off for the day since we were only open through late afternoon. Chuckling, I couldn't believe how fortunate I was to have Linda as my baking partner and now our resident teenager Dexter, who provided a laugh a minute. He had joined our team at just the right time, when Linda needed a pick-me-up the most. Uncle Jack's arrest for murder was a dark time, and thankfully, she and I had uncovered the actual killer. Dexter's antics helped us keep a balanced perspective on life. We would have to give his baker training another go soon.

My steady pace prompted my heart rate to drop and allowed me to catch my breath. *Not too bad*, I thought as I patted my thighs, encouraging them. I was ready for a quiet night in with my little kitten, Peanut, who was quickly not so little anymore. While I was away, she had adopted a new game of hide and seek, finding small items she could carry and placing them in hidden locations for me to discover. Her latest antics involved a pile of hair ties and several pens. I swear I saw her grinning the moment I discovered her stashes.

The sun disappeared, leaving a slightly darkened sky as the streetlights came on. My little cottage wasn't far, and I was grateful that I could walk almost everywhere I needed to in town. But I couldn't get the discussion with Fiona out of my head about buying a car. A vehicle would provide more flexibility in road trips. Her bug was cute, but I had my eye on a chili red convertible Mini Cooper. That never would have been a practical car living in Boston, emphasis being on the word practical. But now I could justify it by living in a beach-side, tropical town. Not that I needed to account for my decisions to anyone.

Rounding the corner of the carousel mall toward the last stretch before I was home, I stopped dead in my tracks. Cruising down Main Street, a red car almost identical to the one off the cliff, and that of the resort employee, passed by. With their left rear bumper smashed. Was I hallucinating from lack of oxygen due to my run? How could I keep seeing the same type of vehicle with comparable damage? I shook my head and rubbed my eyes, glancing up. Yep. Same car. This was getting weird, and no coincidence, given the small population of our town.

Maybe Barney could make some sense of it. I needed to share my observations without letting on about my investigation, since he frowned upon me getting involved. I pulled out my phone to check the time. Hopefully, it wasn't too late for a visit. And extra time would allow Peanut to do her thing. I had left several small drink umbrellas in a pile on my living room side table for her hiding game. They remained for several days, and I wondered if tonight would be the night she hid them.

Picking up my pace to a light jog, I headed to Barney's.

CHAPTER SEVEN

As I neared the north end of Main Street, I could again hear the music coming from Fiona's and wondered if that annoyed the residents. Personally, I felt it was a nice touch that contributed to a lively, upbeat atmosphere, and I was all about the positivity. I slowed down to look both ways before crossing the street. Barney's house wasn't far, but most things in Belle Harbor weren't far from anything.

I walked along the street, keeping an eye out for cars, as there were no sidewalks. Barney's place was a cottage-style, larger than mine, with a picket fence around the front. I noticed the flower beds were a little overgrown as I turned down the gravel driveway to a light and some noise coming from the back. The standalone garage had the door wide open, overhead lights on as if it were an operating room. Barney and Uncle Jack had their heads buried under the hood of Barney's old-time pickup. Tools clanked against the engine, along with quiet conversation.

There was no way not to startle them from their concentration. "Hi guys," I quietly said from about ten yards back.

Uncle Jack whipped his head around with his hand on his heart. "Tilly," he said and approached me for a peck on the cheek, grabbing my hand. "How are you?" He glared at me with furrowed brows.

Squeezing his hand and letting go, I replied, "I'm good. Just had a short run to get back into the swing of things. That helped." I stepped around the truck and said, "This is a beauty."

The shiny burgundy truck looked brand new. Barney must have taken exceptional care. "She's just about ready for the parade tomorrow," Barney said, rubbing the fender affectionately. The Dugle family from the larger neighboring town had a private collection of vintage cars that they brought out once a year as a fundraiser. The owner had built a successful waste management business and used much of the proceeds to rescue and restore a coveted collection of vehicles. Along with the parade, they held a car show and invited any owners of classic cars to take part.

"I'm a little surprised you let it out of this cocoon," Unkie said, waving his arm around the garage.

Barney had finished the garage to look like a living room, including heat. "She's meant to be shared," Barney replied, beaming with pride. "Tilly, would you like to ride along?" he asked.

"Nah, Justin and I plan to watch together. Tell me about this." I suspected with my request I may have just committed myself to an hour or so with these motor heads. Barney shared how he had acquired the 1952 Ford truck about ten years ago from the barn at an old farmhouse. He had lovingly restored it over time to its current state. I walked along the wall to the back, where I found the bed of the truck lined with beautiful wood. The wheels practically sparkled in the bright lights.

"Now we just need to get this old guy the car of his dreams." Barney jabbed Uncle Jack in the arm.

Grinning, I said to Unkie, "Do tell."

He slightly bowed his head as he said, "Maybe someday. We have a lot going on right now."

"There's no time like the present," Barney said. "I may even have a lead on one for you. And I don't think it will need much work."

Uncle Jack stepped out of the garage and ran his hand through his hair. "Double teaming. Not fair."

"And," I started as I followed him, "what would Linda tell you to do?"

Holding his stomach as he laughed, Unkie said, "I never had a chance, did I?" Stepping toward Barney, he said, "Alright, hook me up."

I loudly squealed and clapped.

"It's going to be a nice addition to the local collection," Barney said, pointing at me. "Tell her."

What were those two cooking up? I looked back and forth between Barney and Unkie as they paused.

"All right. It's a 1956 Studebaker Golden Hawk. Just like Mom had when she carted us kids all around many years ago." Uncle Jack sniffled. What an incredible tribute to the woman who inspired this. Grandma Luna's influence had extended well beyond her passing many years ago. I wished with all my heart she could see us now. Unkie getting married to the love of his life, her granddaughter opening a bakery and cafe in her name, selling her signature cream-filled cupcakes. The prickles on my arms stood up as I rubbed them.

"I can't wait to see it," I said, giving Uncle Jack a huge squeeze.

"Enough mush. You didn't come here to talk gears and wrenches," Barney said.

"It's probably nothing," I said, wiping my sweaty hands on my shorts. My nerves engaged when I had to share with Barney that I had been investigating on my own, never knowing how he would react.

He would describe it more as snooping, and I was sure he was mostly worried about my safety as some of my previous situations had become a little precarious the closer I got to uncovering mysteries.

"Doubt that. But you know how I feel about your involvement," Barney said. Yes, grateful for my insights, but concerned about my well-being.

"Just have an observation right now. Nothing else," I said, looking at Uncle Jack. He wasn't in favor of my nosing around either. "You know the color, make, and model of the car that went off the cliff?"

"Yes." Barney slowly drew out the word, as if trying to figure out where my thought process was going.

I hesitated, pondering whether I was making up scenarios in my head. Sometimes our thoughts convinced our brains that events were real, when in fact they were not. Watching a 3D movie was a perfect example, like when something flew at your head and you ducked. Pandora's box was open and there was no closing it now. I would just share what I saw and Barney could do with it what he needed for the official investigation.

"I've seen at least two more like it with almost the same damage," I said. There, done.

Barney moved to the side of the truck, rubbing his chin. "Hmmm," was the only sound he made.

"Ha. I knew it. There's something going on specific to the red car, isn't there?" I prodded.

"I hate to admit it, but I think it might relate to an unsolved case from a while back. An accident where the woman died, but we never discovered the cause." Barney pulled out his phone and walked toward his house, pointing to the door. "I'm going to call Deputy Stevens to pull those cold case files."

"Tilly, be careful," Uncle Jack said. "We don't know who is doing this or why."

"Of course," I said. "I don't think I'm in harm's way as long as I don't have that same type of car."

Emerging from the house, Barney said, "Let's get back to the final touches, Jack."

Waving, I began a slow jog away, relieved I may have provided information to move the mystery along. My curiosity would certainly nag me to find out more. I couldn't rest until I connected the dots, and I could see the resulting picture. Time to pull out my notebook when I got home and jot down the clues and my questions.

The sky was now a much darker blue than when I stopped at Barney's. I neared my cottage to see my automatic timer had turned a small lamp on in the living room. I let myself in with plans for my evening to diagram out the crime and clues while I ate dinner. When

I opened the door, my glance pivoted toward the light and the table where the umbrellas used to be. OK, Peanut. Game on.

CHAPTER EIGHT

J ustin unfolded the lawn chairs and placed them next to each other in front of my cottage. He gestured for me to choose. The parade would start shortly and it wouldn't last long.

"The benefits of having my own business," I said. "I can close a bit early to partake in community activities." This morning Dexter and I gave the muffin batches a second shot. He had his game face on the entire time. The concentration and seriousness were admirable, but it made it tough to keep a straight face. I could just hug that kid to pieces for his commitment. I snickered.

Justin leaned back in his chair and stared at me. "Glad to see you relax a bit. I was pretty worried about you after the accident."

"Yeah, that was horrific. I'm trying to focus on what's in front of me, and any clues I can think of," I said.

"I know your brain. You have that percolating on the back burner," he said. "Anything I can do to help?"

Shrugging, I said, "Not sure. There's just nothing obvious popping up. No matter how many ways I look at it."

"It's possible, Tilly, that we may never know," he said.

I shuddered in a breath, unwilling to accept that scenario. A person died, and I couldn't let that go until I exhausted every thought path.

The sound of chairs being placed on the ground from my left side startled me as Uncle Jack and Linda joined us to watch the parade of cars. Unkie held the seat for Linda, then rubbed his hands together like he was anxious for this to get started. He winked at me and slightly dipped his head, a secret behind that expression. That man loved an adventure and regularly tried to get me to stretch my comfort zone.

"Hey kids," Unkie greeted as he sat next to Linda and grabbed her hand. "We have some news." He pulled Linda's second hand into his grasp and gazed lovingly into her eyes.

What in the world could it be? They were already engaged. I highly doubted adopting kids would be in the picture at their age. Did they run off and elope? I glanced at Uncle Jack's ring finger, but Linda's hand hid it.

"Jack, stop teasing them," Linda said.

Releasing her hands and pumping his arm in the air, he said, "I'm getting a Studebaker!" Well, from his excitement, it was kind of like a baby for him.

"A what?" Justin looked at me, brows furrowed.

"A car," I answered. "One just like my grandma Luna had. I can't believe you found one so fast." I turned toward Unkie.

"When the timing is right and you're motivated, taking action makes things happen." Uncle Jack chuckled. "It's not too far from here and in pretty good shape."

"Congratulations," I said as he beamed at all of us. Now that was living your life to the fullest.

Turning toward Linda and us, Unkie exclaimed, "How about a road trip to pick it up?" He bounced in his lawn chair, and I expected it to collapse from the motion.

Reaching my hand to his arm to settle him down, I said, "The last trip we took was a bit too much excitement for me." A brief vacation on the Coast Excursion train had resulted in getting embroiled in a family drama to the degree that one of them ended up dead. Somehow, I found myself smack dab in the center of the mystery and in danger. I shuddered, thinking of the possibilities if that hadn't turned out so well. Surely a car trip would be uneventful. Drive to the destination, maybe stop for a meal, head home. "I'll have to figure out a schedule for the bakery, but yeah." I looked at Justin, who nodded. "OK, we're in." The opportunity to see the joy on Unkie's face when he was actually in the car's presence would be priceless.

From my peripheral vision I saw movement on the opposite side of the street. "Justin," I whispered.

Following my line of sight, he leaned over to me. "He looks eerily similar," Justin replied.

The man with two young kids in tow was the spitting image of the guy who was driving the SUV. They scouted out a location to watch the parade and grabbed a seat on the sidewalk directly across from us.

"Uncle Jack, do you know him?" I asked quietly, not wanting my voice to travel.

"Tilly, I know what you're thinking," he replied to my unasked question. "It's not him."

As if sensing our conversation, the guy raised his hand and waved. "Hi Jack," he hollered. His two little ones mimicked the gesture. Neither of them could have been over six years old.

"That's Aaron. His wife was killed in a car accident about a year ago," Uncle Jack explained.

"How can you be so sure? That's motive enough right there. Did they find out how it happened?" I asked, sure this line of questioning would prove fruitful. It was too much of a coincidence to be nothing.

So many more questions. I wanted to rule him out as a suspect but needed to be unemotional about it.

I squeezed my eyes closed. This puzzle was rapidly becoming complicated and messy. The sound of engines roaring came from far down to our right. The parade was about to start. Deputy Stevens emerged from our far right, walking down the middle of the street, leading the cars. The spectators stood and pointed as the first car came into sight.

Justin held my hand, squeezing, knowing I was preoccupied with the revelation of Aaron's circumstances. Cars honked and flashed their lights. Barney and his shiny pickup were first, his parade wave in full force. He had a passenger doing the same thing, and as they got closer, I saw Florence widely grinning and throwing handfuls of candy to the kids along the parade route. She owned the bookstore next to Uncle Jack's Checkered Past Antiques shop and was quite stoic in her expressions, except when she was around Barney. Two unlikely partners, but somehow they had great chemistry, bringing out the best in each other. Might there be another wedding soon?

I elbowed Uncle Jack and pointed at the shiny red truck as it rolled by. "Double wedding?" I suggested.

Unkie snorted. "Don't think I haven't suggested it," he said. "All in due time. Maybe mine and Linda's wedding will be the impetus for him to propose."

My brain drifted into a trance as the vintage vehicles slowly ambled past, and I tried to envision Aaron behind the wheel of the SUV. With all my heart, I didn't want it to be him, and I believed Unkie. But I had to uncover evidence to support it, and somehow find the actual killer.

CHAPTER NINE

T he hostess seated us at a booth near a corner away from the entrance. Justin and I plopped into the faux leather seats as they squeaked. I hoped for distraction but suspected we would dive into the details of the investigation.

"Hi guys," Fiona greeted. "What can I get you?"

Glancing at Justin and shrugging, I said, "I've got decision fatigue. Why don't you choose?"

Justin grabbed the little drink menu from the display to his left, running his finger down the list. He grinned and looked at me. "Let's having the Screaming Red Zombie."

I was up for anything from Fiona's, yet to have anything to eat or drink here that I wouldn't have again. Plus, what a fun name for an adult beverage. I didn't know what was in there and I didn't care.

Placing two drink napkins on the table, Fiona said, "You got it," then turned and left.

I leaned onto the table and smiled. "Thank you. I just want you to know how much I enjoy being with you." In my former life, I would never have expressed my thoughts and feelings as much as I did with Justin. And even with Uncle Jack. After over forty years on the planet, I finally felt like I had found my people and was coming out of my shell. Better late than never. Life wasn't always easy, and I didn't expect it to be. My choices were more about becoming the person I was meant to be and surrounding myself with supporters who encouraged revealing my authentic self, rather than detractors or saboteurs.

"Tilly, it warms my heart to the ends of the earth to see you happy," Justin said. "Whoops, I think I mixed my metaphors." He chuckled. His easygoing manner and acceptance of himself was such an excellent model to follow.

"Don't think I've forgotten about open mic night," I said, wagging my finger at him. "Why don't we pick a date right now to get it on the books?" I grabbed my phone and swiped to my calendar. Memories of our first time at the comedy club flooded back from our first official date. I showed the calendar to Justin. "What do you think?"

"I think one of these days we may have to be a duo up on that stage," he said. I waited for the punch line, but he was dead serious, not blinking as he stared at me.

Pulling the phone close to my chest, I shook my head. "Not in a million years. I'll cheer you on from the crowd." I wiggled in my seat at the thought of standing on stage under a spotlight, faces from the audience expecting to be entertained. The night we went to the club, the crowd was friendly, but I imagine that wasn't always the case. My ego couldn't take that.

"Zombie's up," Fiona exclaimed as she set two hurricane style glasses in front of us with a blended mixture of orange and red liquid, topped by a slice of pineapple and a maraschino cherry. "Did you tell Justin about the car?"

"Oh no, are there more clues?" he asked, hand stopping mid-way to grabbing his drink. "What about the car?"

"Sorry, did I spill the beans?" Fiona asked, holding out her hand in a halting manner.

Shaking my head, I replied, "No."

"Oh good," she said.

I held both my hands up. "No to Justin's question. Yes to yours."

"I'm confused," Justin said, looking at Fiona. "What about a car?"

"OK. One thing at a time." I took a swig of my drink, another winner in my book. "First, I'm thinking of getting a car," I said to Justin.

"Awesome! What kind? An oldie like your uncle's or Barney's?" he asked.

"Ha ha. I would be in way over my head with something like that. Although I'm sure I would have lots of help to maintain it." Driving a classic car, especially one as nice as Barney's would send my nerves through the roof. As reckless as some drivers were, I could never relax and enjoy the ride thinking about someone dinging up my paint at every turn. "I want to get a Mini Cooper." There. I said it. I put my desires out for all to see and comment on, bracing myself for remarks about practicality, responsibility, and all the other *ibilities* I expected in response to my decisions.

"That's great!" Justin said. "Let me know if you want me to go with you to get it."

This experience was so new for me, not being concerned about others' feelings but choosing those things I wanted in my life. I hoped that discomfort would wane over time as I took baby steps to boost my confidence.

"What about the clues?" Fiona interjected.

"Fiona, it's not going well," I said. "I thought I saw the guy at the parade, but Uncle Jack insisted it wasn't him."

"Who was it?" Fiona directed her question toward Justin, who had lived in Belle Harbor much longer than I had.

"Aaron Handy," he replied.

Shaking her head, Fiona said, "No way."

"That's what Uncle Jack said, but how could he know for sure?" Sometimes the suspect hid in plain sight. And just because he had two young kids didn't mean he wasn't a killer.

"They were at Disney World and just got back yesterday," Fiona replied.

I sat back in the booth. "How do you know that?" I quizzed, hoping this certainty would eliminate the widowed father from my list.

"He was in here with the kids and that's all they could talk about," Fiona said.

I blew out a breath, my muscles releasing some tension. It was good to know the father was not responsible, but someone was, and I felt farther away from uncovering that answer.

We provided Fiona our food order and she scooted off to the kitchen.

"Justin, I feel like every piece of information separates us even more from the truth." For the first time, I accepted we may never find the person who did this. A murderer might just get away with the crime. Did they live in Belle Harbor? Did we know them? I shuddered, committing that I would not let this go. I couldn't.

"Do you think it could have been a tourist?" Justin asked.

"I'm torn. On one hand, I hope it is so that they aren't hanging around, menacing Belle Harbor. But then they may never pay for their crime. On the other hand, if they are local, then..." It was unfathomable that someone in town, that we knew, could have done this.

Reaching for my hand, Justin said, "I know that action can get you out of your head and away from the spiraling thoughts."

If I didn't believe in soulmates, I was beginning to. Justin and I hadn't known each other in the big scheme of things for all that long. Yet his perception of my behavior was pretty darn accurate.

"OK." I chuckled. "You probably know what I'm going to say."

"Let's do it tomorrow after work. The angle of the sun will be different, but it's the closest we can come to simulating events," Justin suggested.

Appearing at our table, the waitress placed our meals in front of us. I was adventurous in changing up my beverage, but give me the smoked macaroni and cheese all day long. The bowl with lightly

browned crunchy topping steamed in front of me, ready to comfort.

CHAPTER TEN

I slowly brought the cupcake to my mouth, inhaling the vanilla scent as I briefly closed my eyes for a taste. I deliberately steeled my expression so I wouldn't discourage Dexter from his next baking accomplishment as I prepared to sample his first attempt at our signature cream-filled cupcakes. The smell was wonderful, and I desperately hoped the taste was too.

Opening wide, I dove into the treat so that I would get some of the piped-in cream in my bite. The soft white mixture squeezed out, touching my nose. My eyes widened.

"Oh no. What's wrong?" Dexter stepped toward me and grabbed a cupcake, examining it from all sides, his slack expression questioning my reaction.

So much for being non-demonstrative with my face. Poor kid. "No," I started, reaching out my hand. "They are amazing!" I took another huge bite to prove myself. "See?" I mumbled with a mouthful of cupcake.

"You're just saying that," he mumbled, taking a bite of the cupcake in his hand. His eyes widened and he grinned from ear to ear, cupcake plastered across his teeth and falling from his mouth. He swiftly closed his mouth and swallowed what was inside. "I'm so sorry." He grabbed a paper towel and swept up the mess he had made on the floor, tossing it into a nearby trash can. He grabbed another cupcake. "They're pretty good, aren't they?" he said, popping the entire thing into his mouth.

"Dexter, you outdid yourself. They are worthy of being sold to customers," I replied. "Even better than Uncle Jack's first attempt." I would never forget Unkie's help, resulting in shortening being used for the inside cream. And neither would he.

I paused, glancing around the kitchen where it looked like every utensil and ingredient were on the counter. The entire surface was covered in a light dusting of flour, Dexter forgetting to turn the mixer to low as he poured in the dry ingredients. A cloud emanated from the bowl, covering him and turning his dark hair a light gray.

He rubbed his head, creating another swirl of flour around him. "I made quite a mess, huh?" He glanced around, picking up some empty bowls and heading toward the sink.

"It's all a learning process. I'm sure you'll get more efficient over time," I encouraged him. The kid had a lot of potential, and it started with his great attitude. Someday I expected he would move on to other things in his life, but for now I was grateful for the youthful presence.

The door from the lobby swung halfway open, Linda peeking her head through. She looked at me to gauge what her response should be at the scene she had just encountered.

Nodding, I held out another cupcake to show Dexter's success at baking. "He nailed it," I said, taking a big bite.

Linda fully entered the room and approached Dexter with her hand held high. Dexter slapped it. "Thank you both for the opportunity. I've already learned a lot," he said.

"As long as you're baking, you sure have job security as a dishwasher," I teased him. There was about twice the amount of work as when Linda and I baked.

"Tilly." Linda moved to my side, away from Dexter as he grabbed the dishwashing sprayer and she handed me a napkin. I may need to install a mirror in the kitchen so we could check our faces for dessert crumbs. "Monica is here."

"Oh," I said. "Is everything OK for the catering?" That's all we needed, some kind of problem with the wedding plans.

"Yes, it's fine. She asked to talk to you," Linda said.

"Did she say why?" I asked.

Linda shrugged. "I couldn't get anything out of her," she said, raising her voice over the din of Dexter's clanging of pans.

"Sure, send her back," I said, gathering up a batch of dirty dishes and depositing them next to Dexter.

I wished my thought didn't automatically go to a place of doom, but I couldn't help it. Grabbing a towel, I began wiping down the work surface to prepare for another batch of dessert.

"Hi Tilly," Monica greeted as she joined us in the kitchen. Linda shrugged behind Monica's back and returned to the lobby to serve customers.

Moving to the opposite end of the room from Dexter to avert any errant showers, I asked, "What can I do for you?" with more formality than I intended.

"Well," she started, looking around. "You have a great bakery here." She seemed to be stalling. Was there something she didn't want Dexter to overhear? I suspected he was in his own world, anyway. And this was my kitchen, so he was staying put.

I waited, not uncomfortable at all with the extended silence between us, broken up by sounds of Dexter's work. My radar was up.

"I just had a question for you," she finally continued, glimpsing at Dexter over her shoulder. "I was just wondering why you were so interested in my car at the resort the other day when you were visiting."

What? That question was from left field. Did she make the trip to the bakery merely to ask me about my inquiry into her damaged car?

"Um, it's just like one that got ran off the road the other day. Identical damage," I said.

"But why were you interrogating me?" Monica's tone turned nasty, throwing me off kilter.

"I'm sorry if my question upset you. I was only curious to see if it could help find the person who ran the other car off the road. If maybe you saw the person who did it." Maybe getting her onto my mission would soften her stance. If she didn't know who smashed her car, and if it was the same SUV I was looking for, she might get some answers.

"I think you're snooping where you shouldn't be," she said, taking a small step toward me. This conversation was going downhill fast, and if it turned physical, I was thankful Dexter was nearby. Did she know the killer and was covering for him?

Holding both hands up, I wracked my brain for what to say to safely exit this exchange. "Got it. The mystery is probably going to remain unsolved."

"Well"—Monica took a quick look toward Dexter—"thanks for your time." Moving toward the door, she opened it, and with a voice as sweet as the cream-filled cupcakes said, "Maybe we can partner on some catering in the future." Then she escaped beyond the swinging door.

That was one of the oddest interactions I had ever had. What was the connection between the car off the cliff and Monica? I was more determined than ever to continue pursuit of the truth.

Dexter's methodical movements in completing his chores provided me some comfort. What would I tell Linda that Monica wanted when she inevitably would ask? I didn't want to worry her unnecessarily about any disruption in the wedding plans, so it would have to be a vague reference to Monica's suggestion about a joint venture. Not in a million years would I choose to work with that woman after how she addressed me. Even if it meant turning down money, nothing was worth that drama.

It felt like she sucked all the oxygen from the room. Thankfully, Justin had agreed to an outing later today to see if we could figure out anything new by visiting the scene of the crime. I really needed that distraction and couldn't wait for the fresh air.

CHAPTER ELEVEN

My backpack felt like a thousand pounds. The purpose of this trip was anything but pleasure, and my entire body felt the weight of it. Justin had offered to wear both backpacks, but I stubbornly strapped mine on, determined to get answers on this trip. We slowly approached the crossroads where we had veered off the official path on our previous visit, stopping at the corner. Still overgrown, as if nobody ever traversed the sanctioned route, Justin pointed that direction. "I think we may have a better view if we go that way this time," he offered.

Initially, I wanted to repeat our steps identically to that of the former hike to replicate the exact experience. Would we be able to gain any new information if we didn't follow the exact path? I trusted

Justin's experience and agreed. "OK." I started through the tangles of vines, stepping high to avoid tripping.

"Tilly?" Justin whispered.

I stopped and turned. "Yes?" My mind was focused on sorting this out. That guy couldn't just kill someone and get away with it.

"Why don't you let me go first? I'll stomp down the path," he said, waiting for me to come out of my trance. "I know this is really bothering you. One step at a time." He squeezed past me and led the way.

"Thank you," I replied, appreciative that Justin always put me at ease.

We continued trudging through the thick brush, the tree overhang above darkening our path and mirroring my glum mood. I had yet to share with Justin the odd visit I had from Monica earlier in the day. I wasn't sure myself how to characterize it. Other than bizarre, and frankly, a little frightening.

Justin deliberately placed himself to methodically choose the safest footing for both of us. He turned and smiled.

"So far, so good," I said.

He returned his focus to the expedition as we finally neared an opening. My heart raced as I anticipated the possibilities. Would this different view enlighten any more clues?

We emerged into a large grass-covered area that looked like a park. The county had obviously been here to put in the bench on a cement slab overlooking the coastline, with the view similar to that from our prior trip. Except this location also had several landscaped shrubs placed around the bench and a rock wall bordering the edge. I imagined this was to keep people from tumbling down the hillside.

Justin slipped his backpack off and gestured for me to turn so he could help remove mine. He placed them alongside the bench and stretched his arms high and to each side.

My back remained to the edge, and I was afraid to contemplate the outcome of this trip.

"Tilly, if nothing else, we can eliminate some possibilities," Justin said, taking my hand and guiding me to the bench.

I shivered, as goosebumps populated my entire body, at Justin's ability to sense my thoughts and feelings, and also at the prospect of gathering more clues about this horrendous crime.

"Let's catch our breath and just take in this incredible view. When you're ready..." he started. The sun was hours away from setting, the waves generating a lot of foam as the tide sped toward the shore. A gentle breeze brushed the trees, providing relief from the heat at this higher elevation.

Justin reached for his backpack, retrieving two water bottles and handing me one. I downed about half the bottle and held it in my lap with both hands, the condensation cooling my bare legs.

"Would you do me a favor and also hand me my notebook?" I asked.

Chuckling, Justin said, "I'm slipping. That should have been the first thing I unpacked."

I exchanged my water bottle with him and opened to a blank page. "It feels like we're chasing a ghost," I said and started making notes about the first trip we had made. Perhaps starting from that point could lead me into a revelation. I jotted down the fact we had taken a different path to the top. Not a clue, but somehow I believed the universe wanted us to go that route for a reason. Closing my eyes, I felt the sun from the other day. It was earlier, and the angle was a bit more to our backs than today. Pinching my eyes firmly shut, I slow-walked my brain through the next steps to remember exactly when we heard the tires squealing and first saw the SUV.

Breathing in slowly, I exhaled to relax my muscles. Sounds came to life, with a few birds serenading us and the whoosh of the powerful waves in the distance and the faraway noise of traffic on the road below. I stood and approached the rock wall to see what visibility we had to the road below. Like before, we had almost the same view: the sharp curves and a panorama of both directions of the road up and down the coast.

From the time the tires sounded before we had seen the complete interaction between the SUV and the car he ran off the road, leaving no doubt in my mind that his deliberate action resulted in the death of the other driver.

As if on cue, the same noise began out of sight to my left. I shook my head, unsure if my memory was so vivid that I was reliving the experience or if a repeat of the events was about to happen.

Justin leapt from the bench to my side. "Tilly!" He pointed down the hill at the appearance of the same SUV as the other day, his right front fender smashed, speeding through the curves at well over the advised limit. The SUV quickly gained on the car in front of him, and I wondered if we were going to see a repeat performance. He laid on the horn, prompting the driver in front of him to swiftly pull off the road into a viewpoint, leaving the SUV driver to race away.

"Justin, I can't believe we just saw that," I said, out of breath and thankful for a different outcome this time.

"Let's sit for a minute and gather our thoughts," he suggested.

My thought was that menace needed to be put away. He had already killed one person, that we knew of. Could there be more victims? I grabbed my notebook and began writing. Even new questions coming to light was progress, and I would take every breadcrumb of a clue. Barney could research other potential accidents that may have happened under similar circumstances. And this guy appearing again led me to conclude he wasn't a visitor, he was local. Could this be his path to work? If we staked out the road at the same time and day, would we see him again? I didn't see any way that would work. Barney didn't have the resources, and neither Justin nor I had the time to sit and wait for what might end up being all day. And even then, he might not pass by. My elation at a break in the case quickly dissipated. For the first time, I accepted the reality that he might just get away with it.

CHAPTER TWELVE

Mira's Serenity Salon was one of my happy places when I visited for hair treatment. I had yet to book the works for a cleansing facial and soothing, relaxing massage. My brain was perennially distracted, and I always came up with an excuse why I didn't have time, which probably meant an even bigger reason to actually do it.

"Right on time," Mira greeted me, holding her hand out to guide me back to her stylist chair. Turning the seat toward me, she held it while I plopped down, a little harder than I intended. She grinned at me in the mirror, teasing, "You're a little overdue," as she pulled her fingers through my hair, examining the color. "What are we doing for you today?"

I always considered a change, something to mix it up, but eventually returned to my blue color. It had become part of my identity and I liked the consistency of it. "Maybe a change some time. But for now, just refresh the color and a trim," I said.

Mira pivoted toward the shelf containing an extensive number of bottles with enough color that she could provide her customers anything along the rainbow. She pulled down two bottles. "Rockabilly Blue it is." Mira got to work as the process needed for my dark hair required a lightening step first to prep it to receive and retain the blue. The time in this salon felt like a sanctuary away from the nuttiness of the world, if only for a couple of hours. And a visit with Mira always lifted my spirits.

"Someday I might change. What would you suggest?" I asked.

Mira painted my roots beneath where she would apply the blue, tipping her head. "You could pretty much pull off anything you wanted. So it's really how much change do you want?" She continued separating small sections of hair and flipping them over as she finished swiping the brush. "If you go full-on color, it's definitely more frequent maintenance."

"Yeah, probably not ready for that right now," I replied.

"Speaking of blue streaks," Mira started, slapping her knee as her bright red curls bobbed around her face. "How is your mom?"

The first visit my parents had made since my move to Belle Harbor turned out to be a huge blessing. I had, of course, stressed about every which way their time here would end in disaster. It was anything but that.

For as long as I could remember, I had been a people pleaser. Not sure why, but likely because my parents, especially my mom, always had unreasonable expectations. I knew now that was the case, but as a kid, I just wanted to do good. Mom had grown up in a very loving, encouraging, albeit alternative, environment with Grandma Luna. And I suspect because of that, she rebelled in the opposite direction. I knew in my heart she always wanted the best for me.

"She's great. And that blue streak you put in her hair while she was here was a colossal hit with her friend group," I said. While my parents had visited, they helped to prepare the space for me to open Luna's Cafe and Bakery. That collaboration began the healing of our relationship, and the rift I likely created in leaving my ex and moving away. It felt like the first time in my life they saw me as an independent, capable individual, forging my imprint on the planet. Their support of me and my goals was huge.

"She was a hoot. I'd love to see her again when she visits next time. Maybe I can talk her into something a bit wilder," Mira offered.

"You just might," I said. "I'm trying to get a trip in before the end of the baseball season when my brother's team is near Boston so I can see them all." My first time venturing back east since… The hurt diminished over time but still pricked my heart when I thought about my ex's betrayal. And to top it off, with an instructor at the culinary school I was attending. It felt almost like choosing to follow my dreams was the best revenge. No matter, in the end, I was certain I got the better end of the deal.

"I'm so proud of you, choosing for yourself," Mira said.

I shrugged. That behavior was still so new, but each decision that fell in line with who I wanted to be gave me more confidence to keep building my habit.

Mira finished the last strand and spun the chair to face her. "What are you not telling me?"

Smiling at Mira, I said, "Busted. I just can't shake that experience of seeing the SUV run that other car off the cliff."

"So you have no idea who it could be?" she asked.

"No. But I believe it's someone who might be local. Justin and I went yesterday to see if we could uncover any more clues. And I couldn't believe the same jerk drove by at exactly the time we were there."

Mira's hand flew to her mouth.

"He was revving his engine to get a car to move over. Thankfully, they did, just in time for him to roar past them."

Mira took a seat in the stylist chair, facing me as we waited for the lightener to process. "I wonder…" Her voice trailed off.

"Do you know who it might be?" I asked, scooting to the edge of my chair, hopeful for any insight that might lead us to identify the killer.

"I feel like I've seen him around. I remember the crunched right front bumper, but I had no idea he ran someone off the road," Mira replied.

"I'm sure it's just a matter of time. I just wish I had more time to do a stakeout along the coast highway where we saw him," I said.

Mira jumped from her chair, saying, "I can go with you! I'd love to be part of catching that scum."

Maybe that was the answer, to enlist several people to keep shifts on a watch so we could finally nab him. I knew Barney didn't have the resources to devote to something like that. And what would be the harm? We would just observe and document what we saw, providing that to the police department for their follow-up.

"That's a great idea. I was thinking if we stationed at the lookout spot where the car went down the cliff, we would have to see him, eventually."

Stepping toward me and lifting a few strands of hair, Mira inspected the progress. "Just a few more minutes, then we'll wash and get your color refreshed." She resumed her seat. "Oooo, this is exciting!"

I felt more optimistic about getting a resolution to the mystery. Finally getting that guy behind bars for what he did would be a tremendous accomplishment. I couldn't fathom how you could go about your normal daily life knowing you had caused severe injury or death to another person. There was no way he didn't know that the car he rammed had plummeted over the cliff. At a minimum, most people with a conscience would stop and call for help, even if they were at fault. I hoped it was just a matter of time before justice was done.

CHAPTER THIRTEEN

Mira's handiwork was magic and always perked me up after my visit, and our strategizing about finding the creep gave me hope. I swung my leg over the seat of the moped and sat, glancing at my appearance in the mirror. I loved my blue hair, but maybe if I started thinking now about a change, I might have the courage to go through with it by my next appointment. Strapping my helmet on, I started up and slowly backed out of the parking spot, giving thanks again to my dear uncle for gifting me the moped to get around when I first got to Belle Harbor.

Turning toward the street, I slowly accelerated as I headed to my meeting with the owner of the Maple Hill Inn. Katie had come to Belle Harbor for a day at the beach with her family and they paid a visit to Luna's Bakery and Cafe. She couldn't stop complimenting our bakery items and gave me her business card, offering to meet for a collaboration. I had learned to take these meetings with a grain of salt, not wanting to get my hopes up. And another business customer would absolutely mean hiring a third full-time employee. While I would love to have more of Dexter's time, in part because of the levity he brought to the place, he had school. Our wholesale business just might get as big as the retail. Would I need another place to handle it all? My stomach fell as I thought about all the work involved in the next phase of growth for my business, unsure if I was ready for that. One step at a time. First a chat with Katie to see what she had in mind.

The inn was several miles away from Belle Harbor, on the opposite side of the ocean and up a hill that provided million-dollar views. Traffic was light, people likely getting dinner with their families.

The moped sputtered, jolting me back and forth as it appeared to be gasping for breath. I didn't ride it much, but I hadn't had a problem with it since that initial purchase, and the seller had made it right by fixing it. Glancing at the gas gauge, I confirmed the tank had plenty to get me to my destination unless the indicator was faulty. I wracked my brain to figure out the last time I had gassed up, sure that wasn't the source of the problem. The moped was slowing down on its own, no matter how much I juiced the engine.

Nearing the lookout where the car had gone down the cliff, I carefully navigated to a safe space as the moped expressed a last gasp. How in the world would I ever figure out what was wrong with it? Thankfully, I knew a couple of motor heads that might talk me through it over the phone or come rescue me, if they could get away. I stepped off and placed the kickstand to hold the moped up, standing back with my hands on my hips, willing the cause of the issue to present itself. I circled the entire thing, bending to look under it, but nothing jumped out. Should I even open it up and risk causing further problems with my ignorance of motor vehicles? A tutorial was in order after this from Uncle Jack on basic troubleshooting. There was not much worse than being stranded by a disabled vehicle.

I sat on a nearby rock, holding my phone, ready to dial up help. Unkie would have a tough time getting away from the antique store on a moment's notice, so I mustered my courage to explore the reason I was sitting on the side of the road with a moped that died. I couldn't make it worse, could I?

I jammed my phone into my back pocket and lifted the seat, seeing two large bolts holding it in place. Taped to the side of the bucket was a wrench. I looked at the sky and thanked my lucky stars. Someone had thought ahead for future problems and provided me with some guidance. I wasn't sure if that wrench came as standard issue or not, but I removed it from the tape and began undoing the bolts. First one off, easy peasy. Number two, however, provided a significant challenge. I rotated to the other side of the moped, trying all angles to loosen that puppy. One last heave and it gave way, causing my momentum to land me on my backside. I looked around to see if anyone spotted my gaffe, glad I was alone.

I stood and wiped the back of my shorts, placing the bolts in my pocket and lifting the seat away from the engine to place it on the ground. Inhaling, I poked my head inside the opening, methodically moving my eyes from left to right to spot anything obviously out of place. More bolts, wires, cables, and things I couldn't even name. Oh boy. All bolts looked snug. Check. I looked all around at the cables next, ensuring each was tightly connected. Did that fix it? I turned the key on, pressed the brake handle and then the yellow button, hoping to hear it come to life. Silence. Pressing on, I next examined the different-colored wires. Several appeared to be properly touching the part they were supposed to be, except a yellow one dangling on its own.

I stood back to gather myself, heart racing, feeling very accomplished with the discovery. Certain that disconnected wire was the source of the problem, I poked my head back into the opening to find its rightful home. Following the pattern of the other wires, I found the location missing its link. I squeezed my fingers around the open ends of the wire to firmly attach it. Jiggling it to be sure it was tight enough to allow me to make the trip to the inn, I gleefully tried the starter again, and it roared to life.

Hesitantly, I turned it off to return the seat and bolt it into place. My orderly way of approaching problems again served me well. I only wished that would enlighten me for solving the murder.

I swung my leg over the seat, pulling out my phone to check the time. The detour took about half an hour longer, so I texted Katie about my delay and that I should arrive shortly. Turning the key again and starting up the moped, I sat tall, relishing my accomplishment. At the same time a loud engine roar materialized down the road to my left. It couldn't be, could it?

CHAPTER FOURTEEN

Watching the approaching SUV, I froze. What were my options? With my phone still in my hand, I held it up to get a video of the SUV. With that speed he might appear as a blur, but it could still be useful to provide something to Barney. Steadying my arms, I followed the SUV's movements as he raced toward me, the damaged right front fender prominently displaying red paint in contrast to the charcoal color of the vehicle. Yep, I confirmed this was totally the guy. As he sped by, a gush of wind wobbled my moped.

I had to pursue this opportunity with the murderer so close. He quickly gained distance as he bombed down the highway, dangerously approaching the curve ahead. Flicking up the kickstand, I entered the road and sped up as safely as I could, only hoping I could keep him in my sights until he made a stop. Tightly gripping the handlebars,

I leaned into the upcoming corner, losing sight of the SUV but still hearing his roaring engine.

Glancing at my gas gauge, I saw the needle almost to the F, grateful that I kept it nearly full all the time, with no telling how far this chase might extend. Coming out of the bend to the straightaway, my heart leaped at seeing the SUV well ahead of me. Accelerating a bit above the speed limit, I bent forward in a racing stance. If we happened upon a police officer with radar, that might just work in my favor to attract attention. My mind now homed in on any strategy I could scrape together to once and for all to catch this guy. I goosed the gas, feeling I could safely accelerate until I reached the looming twist where the SUV was about to disappear.

Just before the SUV vanished, a glint of shiny metal caught my eye at the road up to my left. Barney's old truck pulled out to his right, heading in my direction. He was tapping the steering wheel and looked like he was singing. Glancing in my rear-view mirror, and with nobody behind me, I significantly slowed. Raising my left arm and waving it around, I attempted to get his attention. His head turned toward me and he waved, returning his hand to the steering wheel. Dang! I further slowed and stretched my arm high in the air, circling it around, trusting that my odd movements would be enough to spark his thoughts. *Oh, Barney. If you don't join the hunt for this guy, he will get away.*

I pulled to the side of the road, giving up my pursuit of the SUV, with my only alternative for Barney to take it over. I looked to my right, but the SUV was nowhere to be found, and my shoulders dropped. My gut told me it was only a matter of time before he was caught, but would it be before he hurt anyone else? The other accidents he had caused had only damaged cars, but somebody in the wrong place at the wrong time...

A burgundy streak sped toward me from my left. Barney had gotten my message, and his high-powered old Ford whizzed past me on the hunt for the killer, one arm raised as he flew by. I suspected his gesture was meant for me to hold tight while he trailed the suspect, but he knew me better than to sit by as an idle observer. Not a chance.

I guessed that truck engine might have been almost as powerful as his police car, as he disappeared into the curves to my right, my hope soaring at the prospect of this menace being removed from causing any more destruction.

Jumping onto my moped, I goosed it and followed the search. Approaching the corner, I kept my eyes peeled left and right down driveways as the overhang of the trees darkened the road. Confident I hadn't passed them, I continued, emerging from the arbor tunnel into a long stretch of road that led to the seaside town of Merbeach Landing, the same destination where Fiona and I ended up the other day. Hopeful there might be a repeat pattern from the guy, I continued to scan for Barney's beaming pickup, hoping something shiny from his vehicle would catch my eye.

By now, Katie would wonder where I was, again delayed by this chase. I counted on her forgiveness for my mission and a reschedule for our business meeting. Slowing further as I reached the town, I continued to scan for the two vehicles and listened for any engine noise. My heart dropped, and I gave up any prospect of capture, though each time I saw the jerk, he was closer to being caught.

Discouraged by this attempt, I continued ahead to meet Katie at the inn, steadying my labored breathing. Flipping my left blinker on, I slowed to make the turn into the long driveway that wound through the greenery, up the hill to magnificent views of the ocean. I bumped along the gravel driveway, switching my brain into business mode for this meeting, thinking through what bakery offerings an inn might want to purchase. If the deal wasn't over before I arrived because of my tardiness, I would offer a follow-up visit with a variety of samples. This was where my new car would come in handy, as there was no way to safely transport the baked goods on my moped. I hadn't even considered a business write-off for my new car.

Coming to the large parking lot as I crested the hill, I couldn't believe my eyes. Both Barney and the SUV driver stood on the wrap-around deck of the inn, Katie off to the side, hurrying down the steps when she spotted me.

I sidled the moped next to Barney's truck and removed my helmet, stunned by this turn of events.

"Tilly, I can't believe it," Katie said, gesturing toward the duo on the deck. "I'm so sorry for the commotion." She stood and gaped at the spectacle before her.

"Katie, no apologies necessary. Do you know what's going on?" I asked, wondering what that guy was doing here.

"No. I heard screeching tires when Bryan arrived, so I came out to see what was going on," she said, crossing her arms.

"He works here?" I asked, taking a step back. My theory of a local turned out to be accurate, and thankfully it was just a matter of time before he got caught.

Barney had shackled Bryan in a pair of handcuffs and marched him down the steps just as Deputy Stevens appeared at the top of the driveway.

"Yeah, he's a handyman," Katie replied, her voice trailing off as her body tracked Bryan's movements while Barney led him to the police car.

Touching Katie's elbow, I explained, "He's responsible for running a car off a cliff, killing the driver."

Katie's hand flew to her mouth, tears forming in her eyes as she glanced in Bryan's direction. "Are you sure?"

"Sadly, yes. My boyfriend and I witnessed it while we were out on a hike. And I've talked with a few others who own cars similar to the one he rammed, with identical damage, and they described the same guy."

Shaking her head, Katie replied, "Well, then I'm glad they got him."

CHAPTER FIFTEEN

"Cheers, Unkie." I clinked cups with him as we sat in the coffee corner of his antique shop. Just like old times, catching up with so much transpired since we had had a chance for a long heart-to-heart. The quiet of the super early morning provided comfort from the recent hectic events. With Dexter improving his baking skills, Linda and he had offered to do all the orders this morning so I could spend time with Uncle Jack. My only condition with him was that it had to be early enough so I could return to the bakery to help. I was sure there wasn't much he wouldn't do for me.

"Thanks for taking the time for this oldie," he replied, chuckling.

"You know, it's not out of the realm of possibility for us to be in the same building again for our businesses," I said, peering over my cup at his reaction. No plans were in progress, but I always had my eyes open for space that would allow it. The best times I had were in my little corner kitchen in this antique shop.

"What?" he asked, scooting forward on his chair.

Grinning, I said, "You never know."

"That's true. Who would have ever guessed you would move out here?" Standing to refill his cup, he warmly smiled at me.

Not me, that's for sure. With all of my best intentions for my life, in a billion years I would never have thought I would be where I was. I was grateful for the course of events in Boston, because if not for that...

"I worry about you, though, Tilly," Unkie quietly uttered.

Refilling my cup, I reached over and touched his arm. "You don't need to. Things with Justin are great. Business is great. Katie offered to meet another time to see what she might want to do. All is good."

He shuffled his feet under his chair. Normally, Unkie wasn't this fidgety, nor shy about saying his piece. "That's all good. But getting mixed up with murderers, that's a different story."

"I'm sorry that worries you. I try to make the safest decisions and have a buddy with me." My suspicion was that might not be enough for him, but I couldn't help being in the wrong place at the wrong time.

"That guy Bryan didn't seem to care who he hurt. And I just couldn't—" Unkie's voice trailed off.

We sat in silence, the unspoken thought of a tragedy befalling his niece unbearable. "I promise you I will be careful." I held my cup up. "I didn't go searching for him, but when he went by me on the road, I had to take the opportunity."

"I am glad he's behind bars. What did Barney have to say about all this?" He snickered, knowing full well Barney's stance on my involvement in his cases. Appreciative for the help, but conflicted with a citizen, his best friend's niece, no less, being a key part of the capture.

"Apparently, the guy thought someone in a car similar to the one he ran off the cliff had cut him off a while back," I said.

"So this was road rage?" Unkie raised his voice.

Nodding, I closed my eyes. How could someone take their actions so far that they would take another person's life? Maybe Bryan hadn't intended to kill the person, but what was happening in his life to push his emotions to the brink?

"I need to change the subject," I said, the sadness for the victim settling heavy in my heart. Through no fault of their own, they had been the target of a maniac.

"Well, I have some great news," Unkie said, standing. He paced, drawing out the tension for his reveal. He had so much going on all the time, I couldn't imagine what he was about to share. But to see him almost glowing warmed my heart.

"Stop being so dramatic. Spill it!" I ordered, standing to face him.

He shook out his arms like he was flicking off some bugs. This surprise must be a doozy. I rarely saw him so antsy. My brain raced with potential explanations for his behavior. Had he and Linda eloped? Was it something about his business? He said it was great news, so it couldn't be his health.

"You're killing me!" I tapped his arm, knowing his teasing was part of the fun we had together.

"My Studebaker is being delivered today," he squealed, raising up on his toes like his energy was lifting him into the air.

I rushed him and wrapped my arms tight. This milestone had so much meaning for him, bringing back memories of my grandma Luna and his childhood.

Chuckling, he said, "It's going to take some work, but it's at least running."

"Unkie, I couldn't be happier for you. Will it be ready by the wedding? That would be so magical if you and Linda could drive away in your dream car," I said, clasping my hands together under my chin. There was still a chunk of work to do for plans, but they had made most of the big decisions.

"If I can rope Barney into helping, that's my goal." He beamed, so much joy happening for a wonderful man. He had found the love of his life, and they were about to be married.

Pulling out my phone, I checked the time and for any messages from Linda, sure she wouldn't text me unless the bakery was on fire. What a lovely woman that both Unkie and I had in our lives.

"We should probably take care of those last details for the wedding so that's all wrapped up in plenty of time," I said. In case there was a hitch in any part of it I wanted to have a Plan B because those two deserved perfection.

"What's left to do?" he asked, tipping his head.

"Oh boy, so many details." I laughed. "Um, best man. Tuxes. Do you have a honeymoon planned yet? Final decision on food." I shook my head.

"OK. You're right. Why don't Linda and I have you over for dinner and we can make some decisions?" he offered. "I thought we decided on the catering."

"We sampled, but you need to finalize your choices." Monica had called me after her visit to the bakery, apologizing for her aggressive demeanor. She had not reported her car accident, afraid her insurance rates would go up. Sheepishly, she shared this wasn't the first incident, and she worried I would rat her out. After explaining my interest, her angst somewhat eased.

"I'm so glad we have you to help with this," Unkie said. "Maybe someday I can return the favor when you and Justin—"

Holding my hand up to halt any further discussion down that path, I said, "Hold your horses, mister."

"All in due time, missy. But don't waste a moment dilly dallying when it comes to your happiness," Unkie said.

WHAT'S NEXT? MOUSSE AND MAYHEM

Frozen ravioli, a mountain resort wedding, and business burglars...

Eleventh in the Belle Harbor Cozy Mystery series!

Tilly has one eye on the wedding plans for her adoring, quirky uncle while she is scouting clues in a rash of neighborhood business thefts.

Emotions run hot as shop owners point fingers while the thief's daylight deeds become more brazen. Tensions escalate as a dead body appears, whacked by a bag of frozen ravioli.

Tilly is running out of time to locate the murderer before the wedding. Can she vindicate the long suspect list of family and friends or will she be led down the aisle of no return?

About the Author

Sue Hollowell is a wife and empty nester with a lot of mom left over. Finding a lot of time on her hands, and as a lover of mystery novels, she began telling the story of a character who appeared in her head.

The Chemical Bond is a book about Meredith Markette, a young woman who reluctantly enters into the field of law enforcement when her police officer father is killed in the line of duty. Her quest is to discover his murderer and in the meantime come to terms with a tragedy of her youth.

Will this book ever see the light of day? Maybe. Sue really likes the story and character. And writing that book taught her a ton about the publishing industry. Through this experience she has discovered a love of writing stories, and especially mysteries. She hopes you enjoy her books as much as she enjoys writing them.

Connect with Sue on Facebook at www.facebook.com/sueh ollowellauthor and sign up for her newsletter to stay in touch with all things cozy!

www.ingramcontent.com/pod-product-compliance
Lightning Source LLC
Chambersburg PA
CBHW031752150726
47989CB00006B/2685